The Rabbit's Tail

~€ A STORY FROM KOREA €~

Suzanne Crowder Han

illustrated by Richard Wehrman

Henry Holt and Company · New York

For my mother, Mary K. Crowder,
and my husband, Yunsok Han
—S. C. H.

To Laurel, Anna, Johnny, and Jamie
—R. W.

Henry Holt and Company, Inc.
Publishers since 1866
115 West 18th Street
New York, New York 10011

Henry Holt is a registered trademark
of Henry Holt and Company, Inc.

Text copyright © 1999 by Suzanne Crowder Han
Illustrations copyright © 1999 by Richard Wehrman
All rights reserved.
Published in Canada by Fitzhenry & Whiteside Ltd.,
195 Allstate Parkway, Markham, Ontario L3R 4T8.

Library of Congress Cataloging-in-Publication Data
Han, Suzanne Crowder.
The rabbit's tail: a story from Korea / Suzanne Crowder Han;
illustrations by Richard Wehrman
"An adaptation of a longer version of this story in my
collection *Korean Folk and Fairy Tales*" —Author's note.
Summary: Tiger is afraid of being eaten by a fearsome dried persimmon,
but when Rabbit tries to convince him he's wrong, Rabbit loses his long tail.
[1. Rabbits—Folklore. 2. Tigers—Folklore. 3. Folklore—Korea.]
I. Wehrman, Richard, ill. II. Han, Suzanne Crowder. Korean folk & fairy tales. III. Title.
PZ8.1.H159Lo 1998 398.2'09519'0452932 [E]—dc21 98-16627

ISBN 0-8050-4580-5 / First Edition—1999
Printed in the United States of America on acid-free paper. ∞
Designed by Martha Rago
The artist used acrylic gouache on 100 percent rag
board to create the illustrations for this book.
1 3 5 7 9 10 8 6 4 2

AUTHOR'S NOTE

Korean folktales are populated with a variety of plants, insects, and animals, the most prevalent being the tiger and the rabbit. The rabbit is always portrayed as clever and witty, frivolous and vain, while the tiger is portrayed in different ways. The tiger may be noble, magnanimous, and godlike, or weak, stupid, and conniving.

The Rabbit's Tail is an adaptation of a longer version of the story in my collection *Korean Folk and Fairy Tales*. I studied many Korean and English versions of the tale to compare the structures of the story, the depiction of the characters, and the retelling styles. The versions vary in many ways. For example, in *Folk Tales from Korea*, by Zong In-sob, the story has only two characters, the tiger and the thief, and it ends with the thief in a tree and the tiger running away. The version in Kim Sa-rim's collection, *Kothkam Kwa Horang-I* (*The Tiger and the Persimmon*), has three characters and ends with the rabbit losing its tail. In all versions, however, the tiger runs away, thinking he escaped from the all-powerful "dried persimmon."

This tale is believed to have originated in India, with a monkey as the main character instead of the tiger. It probably came to Korea in the fourth century C.E., when Buddhism was introduced into Korean culture.

ong, long ago, when tigers smoked pipes and rabbits had long tails, a huge tiger lived in a deep mountain forest. His roar was so loud the other animals would hide when they heard him coming. He was so sure of his strength that as he roamed through the forest he would roar out a challenge for any creature to match him.

One year, winter was so hard that there was little to eat. Hunger forced the tiger to leave the snow-covered forest in search of food.

Night was falling fast when he finally crept into the yard of a house at the edge of a village.

He saw a large, fat ox in a stall near the gate. The sight made his mouth water.

He sneaked up to the stall. Then, just as he was ready to pounce, he heard a baby cry.

"Human babies are loud," said the tiger and, being very curious, he crept toward the house.

"Stop crying!" said the mother. "Do you want the tiger to get you?"

"I wonder how she knew I was here," thought the tiger as he got closer to the house.

"Hush! If you don't stop crying, the tiger will get you," said the mother.

"She knows how ferocious I am," said the tiger, puffed up with pride.

The baby cried louder, which angered the proud tiger. "That baby's not afraid of me? I'll show him!" said the tiger, and he snarled outside the baby's window. But the baby just wailed even louder.

"Look! Here's a dried persimmon," said the mother. The baby stopped crying immediately, and sucked on the piece of dried fruit. But this the tiger couldn't see through the paper-covered window.

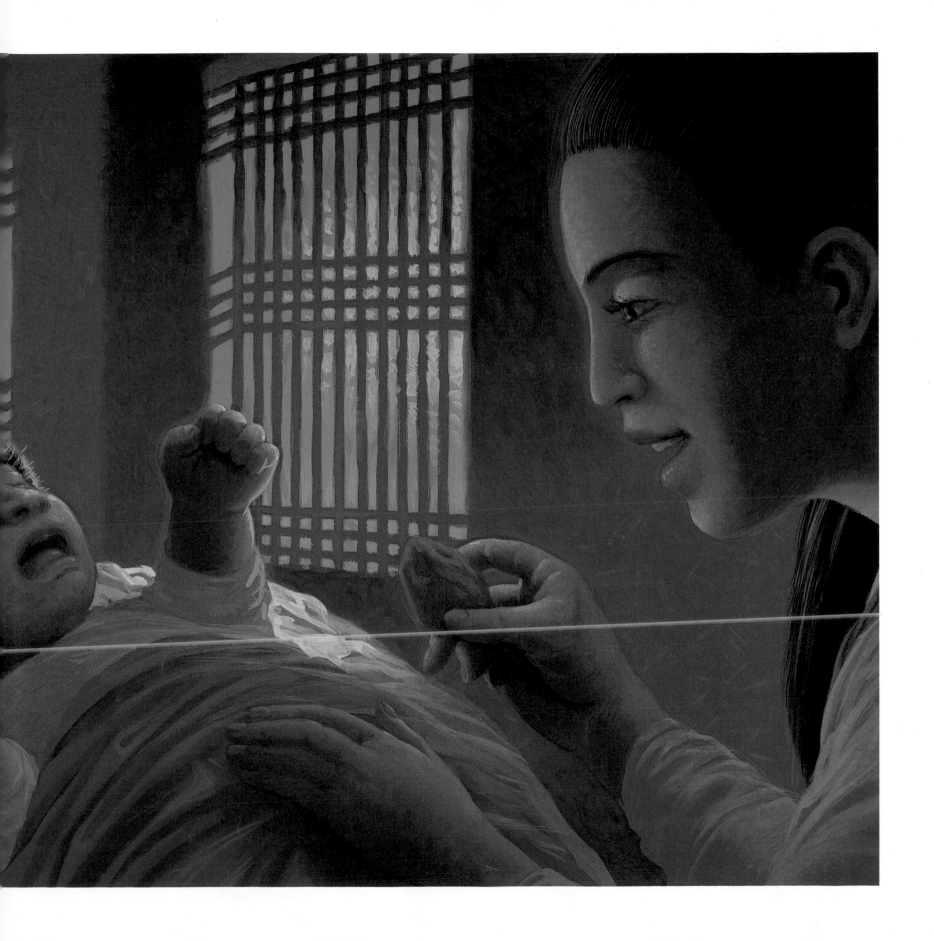

"A dried persimmon? That baby is more afraid of it than of me? It must be really scary and strong, even stronger than I am," said the tiger, and he shuddered. "I better go eat the ox before that dried persimmon gets me."

The tiger slunk into the dark stall and sat down to calm his nerves. At that moment, something touched him.

"Oh, no!" he thought. "The dried persimmon's got me."

"What a nice thick coat. And so soft," said a thief who had sneaked into the stall to steal the ox. "I'll get a lot of money for you!"

Fumbling in the dark, the thief managed to put a rope around the tiger's neck and lead him out of the stall.

"Oh, what can I do?" moaned the tiger to himself. "I can't roar. I can't run or that dried persimmon will kill me. Surely this is the end of me."

The thief, unable to see in the night, was happy to have in tow what he thought was a very fine calf. To get away fast, he decided to ride the calf, and so he jumped onto the tiger's back.

"Strange. This doesn't feel like any calf I've ever ridden," mumbled the thief, and he began to feel the tiger's body with his hands. "It's a tiger!" he cried.

The thief was so frightened, he nearly fell off. "I can't fall. He'll gobble me up for sure," he said, squeezing the tiger with his legs. "I must calm down and try to think how to escape."

"I'm going to die. I'm going to die," moaned the tiger as the thief tightened his hold. "What rotten luck to die at the hands of a dried persimmon! I have to get it off!"

Again and again the tiger shook and jumped and bucked as he ran. But he never once looked to see what actually was on his back. He was too scared!

After a while they came to a grove of trees. When the tiger ran under a large branch, the thief grabbed hold of it, letting the tiger run out from under him.

The thief quickly climbed into a hole in the tree trunk to hide.

The tiger knew the dried persimmon was off his back, but he didn't dare try to eat it. He just kept running as fast as he could deeper into the forest.

Finally, he stopped and let out a sigh of relief. "I can't believe I'm alive. I thought that dried persimmon was going to eat me." He was so happy, he rolled over and over on the ground, laughing.

"Oh, Mr. Tiger," called a rabbit, who had been awakened by the tiger's laughter. "What are you laughing about? It's the middle of the night!"

"I almost died today," replied the tiger. "So I'm happy to be alive."

"What's that?" asked the rabbit, hopping over to the tiger. "You almost died?"

"That's right," explained the tiger. "A horrible dried persimmon caught me. I've just now escaped."

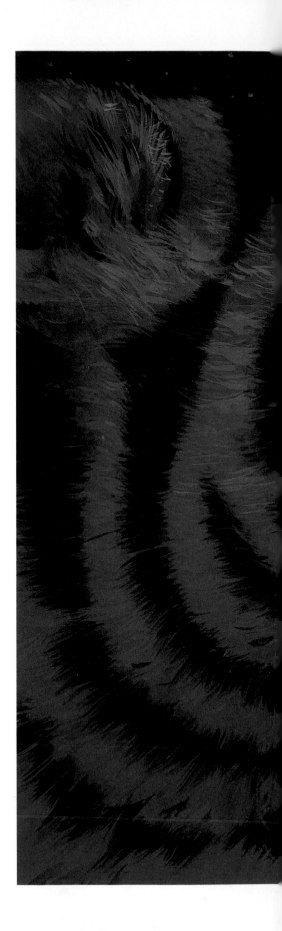

"What's a dried persimmon?" asked the rabbit.

"You don't know what a dried persimmon is?" said the tiger, laughing. "Why, it is the scariest, strongest thing in the world. Just thinking about it gives me shivers."

"Well, what does it look like?" asked the rabbit.

"I don't know," said the tiger. "I was too terrified to look at it."

"Where is it?" asked the rabbit.

"I was running by a large tree when it let me go. I think it must be in that tree," said the tiger.

"Where's the tree?" asked the rabbit. "I think I'll just go have a look at that dried persimmon."

"What? As small as you are, it'll gobble you up in one bite," said the tiger.

"If it tries to grab me, I'll run away. After all, there's no one faster than I am," said the rabbit with a gleam in his eye.

The tiger told the rabbit how to get to the tree. "I'm warning you," he said as the rabbit hopped away, "that dried persimmon is a terrifying, horrible thing. Be careful."

At last the rabbit came to the tree. He looked in the hole in the trunk and saw a man, pale and shaking.

The rabbit laughed.

Later, when he told the tiger what he had found, the tiger didn't believe him.

"Follow me," said the rabbit. "I'll show you." He hopped back to the tree and leapt up to sit in the hole.

"Come on, Tiger," called the rabbit when he saw the tiger slowly approaching. "Don't be afraid. I have the hole plugged."

On hearing this, the thief knew he must keep the tiger from getting to him. He took some strong string from his pocket and tied it to the rabbit's tail. Then he pulled it tight to keep the rabbit from running away.

The rabbit shrieked and the tiger ran. "I told you not
to mess with that dried persimmon," yelled the tiger. "Now
the horrible thing has you!"

The rabbit struggled to get away. The harder he tried to run,
the harder the thief pulled the string.

With one last tug, the rabbit broke free. But his tail was left dangling from the thief's string.

And that is why to this day the rabbit has a stumpy tail.